Adapted by Ann Rhiannon

Illustrated by Joe Moshier

Designed by Stuart Smith of Disney's Global Design Group

A GOLDEN BOOK • NEW YORK

Copyright © 2008 Disney Enterprises, Inc. All rights reserved. Published in
the United States by Golden Books, an imprint of Random House Children's Books, a
division of Random House, Inc., 1745 Broadway, New York, NY 10019, and in Canada by
Random House of Canada Limited, Toronto, in conjunction with Disney Enterprises, Inc.
Golden Books, A Golden Book, A Little Golden Book, the G colophon, and the distinctive
gold spine are registered trademarks of Random House, Inc.

www.goldenbooks.com
www.randomhouse.com/kids/disney

Library of Congress Control Number: 2008924681

ISBN: 978-0-7364-2545-2

Printed in the United States of America

10 9 8 7 6 5 4 3 2

Bolt looked like a regular dog.

But Penny *knew* he was a hero dog.

. . . Bolt found Penny!
And Bolt SAVED Penny!

Bolt really was a **_HERO!_**

Penny took Bolt home.

She gave Bolt a brand-new collar! Now
Bolt was Penny's dog, and she was his person.

And then Bolt's life changed. He was given incredible powers!

Bolt had heat vision and a super bark. He was a super-dog! Penny and Bolt went on lots of adventures together.

BOLT
SCENE 1

BOLT
SCENE 2

BOLT
SCENE 3

And no matter what, Bolt
ALWAYS saved Penny.

For their next adventure,
Bolt and Penny had to save
Penny's father from the evil
Dr. Calico and his nasty cats.

Then Dr. Calico captured Penny!

This time, Bolt could not save her.

But he HAD to try again. Bolt was Penny's **HERO!**

MAILROOM

So Bolt tried to find Penny.

Instead, he got trapped in a box

and mailed far away.

SHIP TO: **NEW YORK CITY**

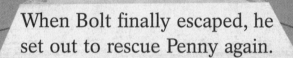

When Bolt finally escaped, he set out to rescue Penny again.

WELCOME TO NY

But where was she?

SHIPPING CO.

Bolt found a cat. AHA! Bolt was sure
that Mittens worked for the evil Dr. Calico.
ALL cats worked for Calico.

Bolt thought Mittens could
take him to Calico's hideout.

First Bolt and Mittens sneaked into a
moving van so that they could get to Penny.

Then they got lost. Bolt got hurt.
He realized that something was
wrong with his amazing powers.
Plus, it was obvious that Mittens
could not find Penny.

HOLLYWOOD

BONK!

BONK!

BONK!

THUMP!

SNIFF!

Mittens did find food. She was happy!

But Bolt was sad. He thought he
would never be able to save Penny.

Mittens helped cheer Bolt up.
They got just enough food to
make them both very, very happy.

Then Bolt met his biggest fan, a hamster
named RHINO. Rhino wanted to help.
Rhino knew all about Bolt. Bolt was his
HERO! Bolt did not understand. How did
Rhino know about his secret missions?

ANIMAL CONTROL

One day Bolt and Mittens had an argument.
She told him that he was not a hero.
He only played a hero on a TV show.

Just then an animal-
control truck pulled
up behind him. Uh-oh!

The truck took Bolt and
Mittens away. Nothing Bolt
tried could set them free.
Rhino climbed onto the
truck and unlatched Bolt's
door. Rhino saved Bolt!

When Bolt realized
Rhino had saved him,
he finally knew the
truth. Bolt was not a
hero at all. He was sad.

Then Bolt decided that he could still be a hero, even without **AMAZING POWERS**. He could be a hero by saving Mittens from the animal shelter.

His plan worked!

But Bolt still wanted to save Penny.

CLEVELAND ★ OMAHA ★ NASHVILLE ★ DALLAS

Washington

Oregon

Montana

North Dakota

South Dakota

Idaho

Wyoming

Nebraska

Nevada

Utah

Colorado

Kansas

California

Oklahoma

Welcome to HOLLYWOOD

Texas

18

At last, with the help of
Rhino and Mittens . . .

Bolt traveled a long, long way. . . .